Henry Possum

Story and Pictures by
HAROLD BERSON

Crown Publishers, Inc., New York

Also by Harold Berson
HOW THE DEVIL GETS HIS DUE
BALARIN'S GOAT

*The text of this book is set in 18 pt. Garamond Light
The illustrations are 4-color pre-separated
ink & wash drawings with wash
overlays, reproduced in halftone.*

Weekly Reader Children's Book Club Edition

Weekly Reader Children's Book Club presents

Henry Possum

One day a mother possum took her five children off her back and lined them up in front of her.

"It is time you learn to play dead," she said, and she rolled over and lay very still on the ground.

"Now you try," she said. And one by one all of her children rolled over and played dead.

All that is, except Henry. He was humming and watching butterflies.

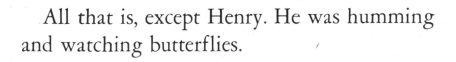

"Henry," said his mother, "come here."
And she gently laid him on the ground
and tried to make him lie still. But it was
no use; Henry kept on humming.

"You'll never fool anyone," she scolded.

"What will you do if a bear comes after you?

Or a fox?

Or a bobcat?"

"I never thought of that," said Henry.

"It could happen," she warned, and she put all five children
onto her back and slowly carried them up into the trees.
"Hold on tight," she said, "you especially, Henry."

As the possum family moved from branch to branch Henry felt
warm against his mother's fur and gazed at the leaves against the sky.

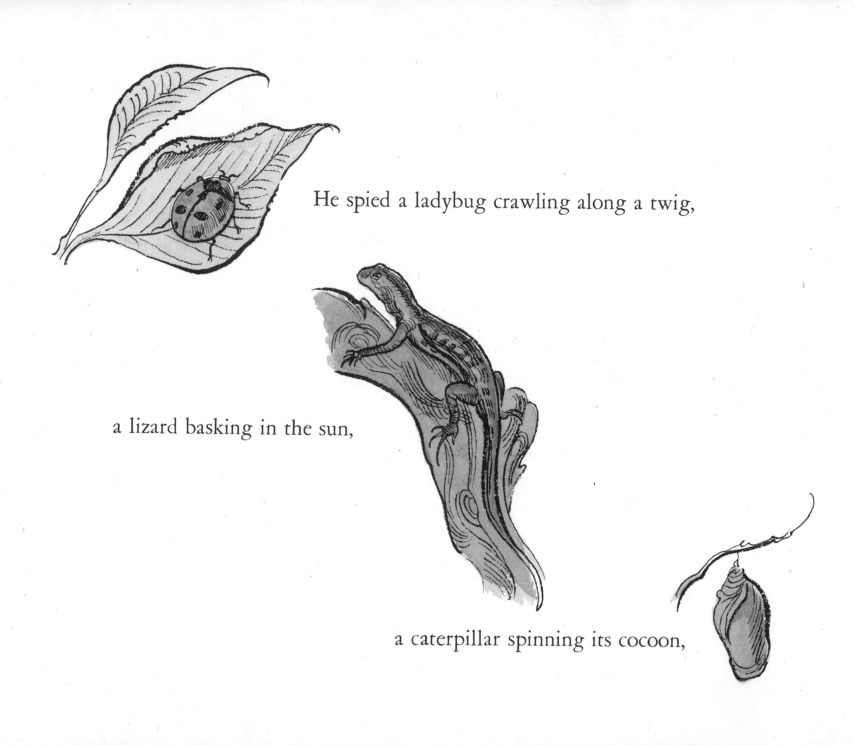

He spied a ladybug crawling along a twig,

a lizard basking in the sun,

a caterpillar spinning its cocoon,

a woodpecker tapping for grubs,   and a squirrel darting through the branches.

Then his twitching nose caught the scent of honeysuckle below them.
It was such a sweet and lovely smell that he stretched down for more,
but he stretched so far that he slid off his mother's back
and fell into the honeysuckle.

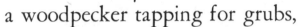

Henry just lay there, enjoying the smell. When he
realized he was all alone, he looked up into the branches,
but his family was nowhere in sight.

Henry climbed out
of the tangled honeysuckle.

He looked around. The woods seemed very large.
As he wandered among the trees,
he began to hum to keep from being frightened,
and the more frightened he felt,
the louder he hummed.

"Well, I never," said a voice to Henry. Henry looked up and saw a magpie rocking on a branch.

"Have you seen my mother?" asked Henry.

"No," said the magpie, "I haven't. But here–take this shiny new flute. It will keep you company. My nest is such a mess that I can hardly turn around."

"You're very kind," said Henry, and he wandered through the woods looking for his mother and tooting on his shiny new flute until he saw a beaver building a dam.

"Have you seen my mother?" called Henry. "No, I haven't," replied the beaver. "I have been busy building my dam. But if you want to play that flute, you'd better learn rhythm like this."

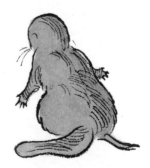

And his tail went slappity slap,

slap,   slappity,   slap,   slap,

against the mud.

"That's wonderful," said Henry, and he went on his way
repeating the rhythm on his flute until he heard
a robin singing in a tree.

"Have you seen my mother," asked Henry.

"No," sang the robin, "but if you're going to play that flute, you need to learn trills like these, Tra-lalalalala, tra-lalalalala, tra-lalalalala."

"Oh, how beautiful," said Henry, and he went deeper into the woods playing trills on his shiny new flute until he saw a bullfrog sitting in a marsh.

"Have you seen my mother?" asked Henry.

"No, I haven't," croaked the bullfrog, "but if you would like to play deep, round notes on that flute, just listen to me.

"Bro-ak, bro-ak, bro-ak," came the deep round sound from the bullfrog's throat.

"That's different," said Henry, and he walked even deeper into the woods until he saw a wise old raccoon sitting in a gum tree.

"Have you seen my mother?" asked Henry.

"Yes, I have," said the raccoon, "she's been looking all over for you. Why don't you stay in one place and play your flute. Your mother will surely come to see who is making music."

Henry found a little hill nearby. He played everything he had learned on his flute—

the beaver's slappity slap, slap,

the robin's tra-lalalalala,

and the bro-ak, bro-ak, bro-ak of the bullfrog.

He put them all together in a song of his very own.
It was beautiful.

The robin and the raccoon, the beaver and the bullfrog all knew
that it was Henry playing his flute and came to listen. The magpie
flew to a nearby tree and proudly puffed her chest. One by one
all the creatures of the woods came to see who was making music,
even Henry's mother.

But a sly gray fox heard the music, too, and when he saw Henry,
he bounded into the clearing. The animals fled. Henry dropped
his flute and fell over.

The fox circled Henry. He sniffed at Henry. But Henry lay perfectly
still, and the fox moved on.

"Henry," shouted his mother as she got up off the ground.
"You learned to play dead!"

"No, Ma," cried Henry. "I learned to play the flute. Listen."

He stood up, took a deep breath, and played as he had never played before. Hearing the music the animals slowly returned to the clearing, and as they listened to Henry's concert, each added his own voice to the melody.